The First War
By

PARRISH WHITAKER

DEDICATION

The First War is dedicated to the dreamers of the world.

When you have a dream but sometimes let fear and

procrastination get in the way think of this book. This book is

for you to walk boldly into darkness without fear. Sing and do

not worry about who is looking at you. Never again put your

dreams to the side, yell as loud as you can

THIS IS MY TIME TO BREAK ALL LIMITATIONS

IN MY LIFE!

CONTENTS

ACKNOWLEDGEMENT

This acknowledgement is for someone special to me and that is my grandmother, Rebecca Robinson. She has been my inspiration growing up. Through her demonstration of strength, the meaning of family and determination; showing me what you can have if you just believe. Instilling in me how God blesses those who believe in him. Encouraging me along the way and telling me that I can achieve whatever I put my mind to. Never to lose sight of my Blessings that come from God. I Miss and Love You Grandma.

INTRODUCTION

"The day the power of love overrules the love of power, the world will know peace". – Mahatma Gandhi.

The First War when asked, many examples come to mind: Gulf War, Vietnam War, War World I, the Revolutionary War etc... All these examples would be wrong. Few have talked about the First War, there is little known. The First War was in heaven when the children of GOD rebelled, and GOD allowed his children to fight. As a parent he watched his children and came into stop the battle at its appointed time.

This is my vision of The First War, the war that never ended…

EPISODE 1- BEGINNING BATTLE

The War of Wars, the battle that could not be explained or understood by any definition. Before evil had a voice or a face there was Lucifer. Given certain favor in GOD's eye, perfect in all his ways; Lucifer's beauty was challenged by none, vanity, and the corruption of power is not just a disease of man but was in heaven. Lucifer and his followers began the process that sealed their fate, a freedom of choice to believe they were above their creator. Once empowered with the courage that comes from the stupidity believing you are beyond the true scope of your authority, the first war has begun.

Lucifer was able to speak with a few angels, his beauty and power gave him a voice in heaven. Lucifer began by speaking on the unjustified glory placed on man by God. Lucifer waves his hand shows the many evils of man. Lucifer ask the crowd of Angels why God holds human beings in such a high regard, they take the blessing given to them and laugh. This moved some of the Angels to question God's glory for the first time. How can an Angel bless with so much beauty and favor speak this way and it not be true? The Angel's began to get angry, and Lucifer could see his plan was working.

Lucifer continues to speak; We are asked to love mankind and forgive man each and every time he fails God. I will speak to God and make him understand man is not worthy of the special blessing and anointing he has placed on them. I ask you to join with me my brother Angel's and demand that God punish man, remove the grace, and love he has shown them. Let them kill themselves without the Grace of God coming to their rescue. We must go to God and force him to listen to us. We are the army of the Lord and have served him faithfully, we must demand he listen to us. We cannot sit idly by while man continues to waste the grace God has placed on them.

Lucifer convinces the group of Angel's to come with him and speak with God. As Lucifer leaves with his group that appears to be a small army, a messenger Angel goes to see Archangel Michael. Michael is the Chief Angel, the leader of God's Army. The messenger Angel begins to tell Michael what Lucifer is planning.

Michael begins to yell for the other Archangels to come and join him. Michael only thought is anger. How dare anyone question God's plan. Michael begins to tell the Archangels that the one who is loved above all has betrayed God. We must stop Lucifer from approaching God. The Archangels agree to stop Lucifer and the other Angels hear Michael call out to come to him.

Michael and the Archangels appear ahead of Lucifer before they approach the gate that leads to

God. The light from the gate is glowing with power and before any of Lucifer's Angels could touch the gate, Michael and the Archangels block his way to the gate ready for war. Lucifer begins to yell at Michael why do you block me from talking to God. Why not join me brother, surely you see that God's faith in man is wrong, God's love for man is wrong.

Michael tells Lucifer to leave and take the Angels behind him with him before it is too late. Michael raises his voice and says again brothers and sisters you are being tricked and do not listen to Lucifer. Lucifer raises his hand in anger and in the blink of an eye, Lucifer and his Army prepare to fight.

Lucifer tells Michael in a loud clear voice where no one can hear. I once put him above all others, showed him Love, and gave him my all. Michael begins to cry and simply ask God to forgive the Angels. Michael hears a loud ringing in his ear, the voice simply says my children ask me to punish man but rebel against my will.

The punishment they wanted for man will be their judgement. Michael hearing these words raises his hand and the Archangels begin to attack the army of Lucifer. Lucifer thinks he is prepared for the battle, but without God's favor he has already lost.

The battle is over very quickly with only Lucifer standing. Michael and Lucifer battle. Michael quickly wins the battle. Lucifer the most loved above us all, how you disappointed our father. Michael rips the wings off Lucifer, and his body falls to the base of Michael's feet. Lucifer's army is laying down, heads bowed in disgrace and shame. They know a disappointed father is looking at them.

It is not for us to question GOD, with all his glory and power. Why he did not sweep Lucifer from the heavens and all his followers immediately, but the end result was the same! The battle was fought and won. The internal flame that once burned so bright inside Lucifer was extinguished and brought forth by GOD's own hand.

GOD engulfs Lucifer with his own internal flame and commanded Michael and the other Archangels to throw Lucifer and his followers from heaven. As Lucifer and his followers fall from heaven and hit the ground, they continue falling into the very bowels of the earth.

The heavenly glow is gone and the descent into the earth changes Lucifer and his Angels into dark creatures, only a distant memory of the glory they once held in heaven. Once they stop falling, they look up and began to yell in rage at all they had lost.

Lucifer shake's his hand in anger and promises to corrupt man, through lies and greed. He promises to show man is not worthy of the blessings given to them. God's favorite creation will be shown as the pitiful creatures that I say they are. God will forgive me, realizing I was right.

I will be welcome back into heaven. Mankind, the one given all of God's love. We will see if you are truly worthy of that love. I will break you, test you and finally make you turn your back on God.

Feeding your need for greed and power.

EPISODE 2 - THE FIRST ARCHANGEL

Archangel Michael looks down through the clouds and witnesses the evil of man. Women and children being raped, abused, greed, and the gluttony of mankind. The hypocrisy being committed in God's name. The corruption of the negative forces taken place all over the world.

It saddens Michael's heart, but that is quickly replaced with rage. A rage that overtakes Michael and brings his anger to a boiling point. The power in his body surges to the top. He can only say one word, ENOUGH!

Michael without a word walk towards GOD and within the time he takes to turn around; he's joined by several Archangels. Each Archangel's wings seem to block the sun when stretched out, each with a sword that simmers with power without being exposed. Their arms and legs vibrate with power that can only come from being favored servants of God.

A beautiful field appears with a lake in the center and there is a rainbow of beautiful people from all nationalities, all ages, happy, singing, and GOD is nestled against a tree surrounded by children laughing as he tells a story. As the Archangels approach GOD, they see the father of heaven long flowing hair with a regal face of authority, yet there is a peaceful aura around him that cannot be explained. GOD stops his story as the Archangels approach and ask why there is such pain in the faces of his Archangels.

Michael says in a respectful voice: Father we weep for your children. The negative forces are gathering to make a push for humanity and their love for you. GOD tells the children he will return in a moment. I must talk with my Archangels, the children sigh, and GOD walks toward the Archangels.

Once he approaches the center of the group GOD's appearance changes. He now looks like a young man in his teenage years, roughly sixteen with long flowing blonde hair and the face of innocence and warmth.

He puts his hands behind his back, looking down towards the ground and shakes his head in disappointment.

With a strong voice that shakes the heavens, he says: Michael do you not remember the price was paid! Forgiveness is an open door that anyone can walk through at any time! The story of humanity has an ending and time is not a factor or concern.

God explains that everyday his children make their own decisions, free will and it is by those choices they will be judged. I love them enough to allow them their mistakes and embrace them with love when they come back.

The Archangel Raphael steps forward: Father as in the Old Testament, you allowed us to visit and proclaim your power and love. Archangel Gabriel: All we ask father is permission to stop the negativity moving without the fear of the power and Glory of GOD.

GOD is walking away and now appears with brown mocha skin and flowing black hair with a hint of gray. Appearing as a majestic King. Body glowing with power that makes the Archangels shake in fear. They immediately drop to their knees and lower their heads in reverence. God turns and looks at them, you can see the disappointment in his face.

The sky and the heavens tremble with his rage; thunder and lightning seem to reflect the anger in God's face. All the children of heaven stop to kneel down in reverence of GOD's almighty glory and at what is about to come out of his mouth.

He speaks: Am I the Alpha and Omega, the beginning, and the end. If I wanted to stop my rebellious children from doing the evil you speak, do you think I need your help?

This is the time of the New Testament; all has been written and what will be done in my name cannot be changed. Archangel Ariel: Raises his head and says softly: Father and Mother God forgive us we only want to bring hope and help your children. Show them the importance of being faithful every day. Encourage them and bring them strength as we did in the Old Testament.

God appearance changes again, now as a woman with short auburn hair, eyes blue as the sea, with a simple wave of the hand the clouds of heaven clear, the thunder and lightning stops.

God smiles as only a forgiving parent would and simply says, rise my children. Heaven rejoices, everyone laughs and plays again. GOD turns to his Archangels and says: The faithful know that my son will return soon. But I have heard some above all other and I will allow you to gather them and lead them to a special place.

I will appear to those few who believe in me and empower them to go out to the world, as I did. My prophets of old, to strengthen my faithful children before my son arrives.

God explains to the Archangels, they will try to stop you but, I will give charge to the ones I love to carry out this mission: Michael, Raphael, Gabriel, Ariel, Azrael, and Uriel you have my blessing, and they disappear. A female Archangel with beautiful wings, dressed as a warrior kneels next to GOD, named: Archangel Jophiel.

Jophiel gather the army, the day of war is not here but a battle is coming. She nods and says yes God, then she fades away. Michael and the other Archangels appear at another area of heaven; Gabriel ask why did we stop?

Michael explains as God said before we are not in the Old Testament. We must change our appearance. With a wave of his hand Michael appears to change, his wings are a blue military styled outfit with a long hooded blue cloak, his sword slides into an opening in the back of the cloak and disappears until needed. Each Archangel follows Michael's lead changing their appearance.

Michael turns to the Archangels and looks at each one with pride. We must not fail. We have been given the opportunity to help man, show that God's love and forgiveness is eternal. All you have to do is ask.

Lucifer will try to stop us. He enjoys each day that man turns away from God. They turn to him for guidance and strength. I once called Lucifer brother and had to cast him from the light. Therefore, he enjoys the fall of man; it brings him joy. I will show man that God's power reigns supreme and to turn away from the darkness. It is not too late. We must make man understand that God will always forgive his children, but he will return, and time is running short for those who deny him.

EPISODE 3 - ANGEL INTERACTION

In New York there is a dark tall corporate building that stands out from the rest of the Manhattan landscape. Inside this building are employees and people conducting business in a normal corporate setting. However, people passing by unaware of what is taking place around them.

There is a secretary sitting at the main desk, which calls out for Mr. Xavier and explains that he is ready to see you now. A six, three-foot man, aged with the face of war, well-groomed black suit approaches the main desk and is directed to an elevator. He goes inside the elevator and presses a button that appears with the letter L.

The back of the elevator wall disappears exposing a massive office with a gentleman sitting with his back turned at the end of a long table. Xavier walks to the end of the table and an envelope appears in front of him. Inside the envelope are seven photos of those chosen by GOD. Without turning around the man at the end of the table simply says, kill them or I will kill you, questions? Xavier picks up the envelope to look at the pictures and simply says, No Lucifer. Lucifer replies, I did not think so and Xavier disappears.

The wall in front of Lucifer changes into a beautiful woman who kneels in front of Lucifer and says he will fail! Lucifer speaks: Yes, Devlin I understand the game well. I want you to make sure he does not fail. Do not question the deed or ask anything about the details, do it! I need not explain what will happen if you fail, Devlin disappears.

Lucifer turns around and his face is as beautiful as it was written but his eyes burn with evil. A cat appears in his arms, and he rubs it and with no one else visible in the room, he asks why are you here? Come to surrender, and Lucifer laughs. Suddenly, a bright light engulfs the room and God appears at the end of the table sipping on a cup of tea.

God appears as a wise older businessman, in a blue suit, with a pair of glasses only to be used for effect. It gives the appearance that he has been vacationing fresh off a coastal island. Lucifer says welcome, and states again you come to acknowledge my glory? With Lucifer displaying an evil smirk on his face. God raises his head and says, well, I see you still have an ego. Your power is less than the trouble it takes for me to sit in this chair. Your time draws near, and you will fail.

Lucifer erupts in anger and throws his cat towards GOD which turns into a massive ball of flame that, engulfs the whole room. GOD raises his teacup, and the flames disappear. GOD laughs and states how did you know my tea was getting cold? GOD laughs again and says, really…really…. really… And continues to laugh which makes Lucifer even madder.

GOD raises from the table and says I see you are having a bad hair day! You REALLY should work on that, then disappears. Lucifer screams echoed throughout the building.

The Archangels land in a small town outside Louisiana. In the distance is an old, rusted church with the echoes of heavenly voices singing praise and worship songs. You can fill the joy coming from the church. Inside the church the pastor is giving a sermon while the choir is singing in the background.

The Archangels walk towards the church, wearing their blue military styled uniform. They enter the church and sit on the last pew and join in singing with the rest of the church.

Next to them is Pamela Cissy Williams an elder mother of the church whose family founded the church. Mrs. Williams is blind but slowly stands up and smiles. She raises her hands to the heavens and says aloud, glory…glory…glory…! The pastor quiets the congregation and says Sister Williams do you have a testimony?

Sister Williams says pastor the glory of the God is here, and his Archangels are among us. The pastor says, they are always among us but unfortunately, we cannot see them with our physical eye.

Archangel Michael stands up and says Pastor in this case you can see us, and the members of the church quickly turn around. Gabriel jokes, way to be subtle Michael. Raphael laughs, Michael subtle never! Pastor speaks, okay son the fun is over good joke. Mother who are these guys? Mother Williams speaks, pastor these are the Archangels of the Lord. Pastor: Okay, by what name do we call you?

Starting with Michael one by one each Archangel introduces themselves. Pastor: Those names are the names of the Archangels. Raphael with a slight irritating laugh, as she told you we are the Archangels of the Lord.

Currently, the doors of the church blow open and Xavier stands in the doorway with several unknown man. Gabriel quickly moves toward the choir and sits down. Xavier says do what is needed and meet me at the next location. Fail me and you will die.

Xavier disappears. Raphael tells the men to leave before they die. The men of Xavier pull out guns and tell everyone to move forward. Michael moves down the aisle way and one of the gentlemen places a gun at Michael's temple.

Ariel laughs and says does your life mean so little you would attack the leader of the Archangels, the general of GOD's army? Leave or you will die this day and forfeit your soul forever! Mother Williams screams, baby please leave and moves to hug one of Xavier's men. She tries to shield him from what is about to come.

As she stumbles forward, tapping her cane. The men move their weapons in her direction preparing to shoot. Michael moves quickly without a thought and cuts and shreds every one of Xavier's men. When it is over, it's just Michael standing with a glowing sword dripped in blood. Gabriel looks up from the choir and simply says we warned you, gotta go, gotta go.

Raphael says, let us spare your eyes from this slaughter and waves his hand and all the bodies and blood disappear. A boy comes forward from the choir and tells Gabriel I serve the Lord. Whatever he needs me to do; I will do for him. I am his faithful servant.

A woman from the crowd screams NO and comes forward and grabs the boy, what are you talking about David? David: I saw this day in my dream mom and GOD has an assignment for me and others Mother. The woman screams and cries, this is wrong why would GOD take you from me?

Gabriel embraces the woman as a comforter and she stops screaming and yelling, suddenly she becomes calm and relaxed. Gabriel in a soft voice says, Mother to GOD be the glory.

You must understand all GOD's children have been given a mission. Blessed is the child who listens to his father. The Mother: I love you and I am not worried anymore. The boy grabs Gabriel's hand. Michael, we have little time and more places. The negative forces already attempting to stop us. Even as we speak, they move onward to the next person.

This child already has protectors, and it will not be as easy to kill the next child. We must be careful, and they all disappear.

EPISODE 4 - PLOTTING AND GATHERING

Xavier appears outside a Japanese Monastery. Xavier yells why are you here? I do not need your help. Devlin appears and says, you could have fooled me seeing how you messed up the last job. I brought you reinforcements. At this time twenty cars loaded with troops appear speeding up the road toward the monastery.

The men exit the vehicle with guns and swords in their hands and kneel behind Devlin. She turns with a smirk on her face and says to Xavier whenever you are ready, idiot. Xavier says WHATEVER and whistles. His men appear dress in red with swords in their hands. The head Monk comes out of meditation inside the main temple.

He tells his Assistants to bring the boys and sound the alarm. A group of boys come in. They look as if they could be brothers similar in height and age. The Monk directs the boys to sit during the room and chant. The head Monk calls out for the chosen Jantai accompanied by four Monks to come forward.

He bends over and kisses Jantai on his forehead. You are the light of justice and do not forget your path my son, now take him away. Jantai cries and is quickly escorted thru a secret passageway.

The head Monk tells his disciples to defend the temple and defend the children. They move toward the front gate. Xavier and Devlin's troops move forward through the gate but are met with strong resistance from the Monks, who have been training for this day. Xavier and Devlin tell their personal guards to avoid conflict, find the child and kill him.

The head Monk and the children remain unphased by the noise and continue chanting. As Devlin approaches the main sanctuary, she instructs the Monks to give up the boy and she will kill no one else.

The head Monk now comes forward and explains, our lives are not yours to end.

The story of our journey has been written by a power greater than yours. Devlin says wrong and projects an energy blast toward the Monk. Without a thought the head Monk waves the blast away like a fly buzzing around someone's face.

Xavier appears behind the Monk and kicks him down the steps, knocking him unconscious. The remaining Monks takes a defensive position around the boys, falling one by one as Xavier and Devlin's army advances toward the main temple. Devlin gets closer to the children and yells in anger, He's Gone! Xavier comes forward and confirms he must have slipped away during the battle.

Xavier tells the troops to retreat and leave the Monastery. Devlin screams, that is it, you will let them live!? Xavier turns to Devlin, do what you want; just meet me at the next location! Devlin turns and looks at the temple where the remaining Monks and children are taking shelter. Devlin with some sick perverted smile blasts the temple as each stone crumbles on the Monks and children.

Devlin's body twitches with an evil erotic sensation, as she looks at the pain and destruction she has caused. After surveying the damage, she smiles then disappears.

The head Monk awakes and directs the surviving Monks to look for remaining survivors along with removing the stones from the main temple. The Archangels appear with the child David. Ariel says we are too late. Gabriel waves his hands and then blows his breath and all that were hurt or killed are now healed.

Michael looks at Gabriel and says brother it is not our place to interfere with the natural order. Gabriel yells back WHAT IS NATURAL ABOUT THIS. Raphael says it is over, let's move on. Raphael disappears and the Monks are making their way through the tunnel with Jantai.

As the Monks escape the tunnel into daylight, Raphael appears and holds his hand out and says come with me. Jantai moves from the Monks and grabs Raphael hand. They reappear with the other Archangels back at the monastery. Michael gathers the Archangels around him with the two boys. I will go to Eden with the boys and prepare the temple.

The negative forces are moving quickly we must separate and gather the rest of the chosen. Michael gives out his directives to Ariel and Uriel assigned to gather two twin girls in Chicago. Azrael and Raphael are assigned to gather a public defender and a prisoner in New York. Gabriel assignment is to go to Norway and convince a young lady to come with him. Michael takes the hands of David and Jantai and disappears.

In a dark abandon building, several gangs are meeting on the upper west side of Chicago. The Dragons, Night Lords two of the largest and powerful gangs in Chicago. They have been expanding their territory without fearing repercussion from the other gangs.

Tommy Banks street name, Baby Killer, Leader of Young Killers, one gang being pushed out of their territory addresses the gangs; this is bullshit. Just because you are the biggest gangs in Chicago doesn't mean we will let you run all the streets.

Shawn Young leader of the Dragons responds by saying, if you do not like it, stop it. Felipe leader of The Night Lords laughs, this meeting is over we got to make money. Anybody got a problem, come see us fool! Devlin interrupts and appears in the meeting. Her beauty catches the attention of all the gang members.

She waves her hand and bags of money appear in front of each gang. Like rats to cheese they rejoice and rip the bags apart. Tommy Banks turns and says we can have money and a party, with lust in his eyes he moves toward Devlin.

Xavier appears in front of Tommy and slices Tommy's head off. His head rolls like a bowling ball coming down an alley towards the gang members. Felipe yells, EL Diablo and everyone pulls out their guns and shoot. Devlin and Xavier just laugh and continue to laugh until all the gang members run out of bullets.

Felipe yells, WHAT DO YOU WANT? Xavier walks up to him, extends his hand and a card appears with an address. It is very simple, kill everyone at this address and I will reward you all with money. Fail me, not only will I kill you all, but I will also kill your family. Felipe yells for everyone to get into their cars and follow him. Devlin laughs and says that went well; then they disappear.

EPISODE 5 – THE FIGHT

Ariel and Uriel arrive in a suburban neighborhood, outside the house of Tom and Diane Williams. The Williams is cooking in the backyard with their sons, John and James. Twin daughters; Cindy and Samantha. Their grandmother; Sarah. Sarah is on the porch laughing and sipping tea enjoying her family.

Ariel and Uriel appear in the backyard; everyone runs to their dad in fear. Sarah comes off the porch and laughs. Is it my time? Have you come to take me home? Ariel says no, it is not your time Sarah and peaceful will be your journey home but not today. We are on a mission from GOD. We need the girls.

Tom yells, the HELL you do. My children go with you over my dead body! Uriel moves forward and says be careful what you ask for. Sarah tells her son it is okay; they are Archangels of the Lord. Tom says, yes right! Diane grabs her children and says let us go! Move! Cindy and Samantha stop and turn around.

Cindy tells her dad it is true; I am not scared. Samantha and I must go with them daddy. Samantha says, we shared this dream but never told you we seen this day coming in a vision. Uriel says they are coming! Ariel says yes, I can sense that danger is coming close.

Uriel leans toward Ariel and whispers, if we leave them, they will die. Uriel tells Ariel to take the girls and I will protect the family. Ariel grabs the children and they disappeared.

Uriel tells the family to go into the house, lock all the doors and windows and do not come outside until it's over. Uriel goes out front and waits in the street. Ahead of Uriel is a line of cars coming down the street. Felipe sticks his head out the window and yells kill this fool! Echoes of gun shots ring throughout the neighborhood.

Uriel hits the ground. You want to be servants of Lucifer, let me help you with an introduction. The blows from Uriel make the ground in front of him break apart and crumble. Each car falls into what seems like a bottomless abyss.

The screams from the car, sends chills throughout the neighborhood; until you cannot hear the screams anymore. Uriel waves his hand as if nothing happened. The neighborhood has been restored. Uriel appears in the bedroom with the family and says it is over. Before leaving he smiles toward Sarah and says Rejoice, my child your deeds on earth will be your reward in heaven.

Raphael and Azarel appear in a crowded, noisy New York Public Defender office of Janice Montez. Below in the main lobby, Xavier and Devlin arrive with their men. Upset with their failure in Chicago. They order their men to kill everyone in sight.

The security officers at the main desk try to stop the onslaught but died quickly. Devlin looks at the chaos and smiles in pleasure. I have the office number it's on the 6th floor. As they all move towards the elevator. Azrael explains to Ms. Montez we must go!

Xavier and Devlin make their way up to the six floors. Killing anyone in their path. Azarel explains to Ms. Montez you must trust us, there will be a battle soon and we will protect you. Azarel turns to the people in the office, he let his wings free to show the true glory of an Archangel of GOD. He tells everyone in the office to leave and go down the steps.

People run out of the Public Defender office in chaos and fear. Some run towards the stairs. Others run towards the elevator. All that run towards the elevator die instantly. As the elevator door opens. Ms. Montez runs between the angels out of fear and out of the office towards the steps.

Xavier and Devlin order their men to kill her. Before they can shoot, Raphael and Azrael shield Ms. Montez from the bullets being fired in her direction. Gabriel appears with his trumpet in hand and blows an angelic note that calms everyone in the building.

The trumpet has such a force it blows Devlin, Xavier, and all their men through the building wall and outside to the ground below. Gabriel tells Azrael and Raphael take the woman with you, pick up the man and meet Michael in Eden; I am needed in Norway. They all disappear.

When Azarel, Raphael, and Ms. Montez reappear they are now on Ryker's Island. They are now in the jail cell of John William Strong, convicted of killing his friend while drinking and driving. Azarel yells at John, you have been forgiven and you are needed. John cries and reaches for Azazel's hand.

Before he can grab his hand, his jail mate Christopher Simons a convicted pedophile explains; He is not going anywhere unless we go together then sits up from the bottom bunk. Raphael tells Azarel grab the woman and move. Ms. Montez asked what is going on? Azarel laughs, I have seen this look before, let's just move out of the way.

Raphael grabs Christopher Simons from his bunk, lifting him high in the air. He says just as easily as you have taken the innocence from children, I now take your life. Raphael throws the man against the cell door. His screams are echoed throughout the prison block.

The only sound more horrifying is the shattering of his bones against the prison door. The door explodes forward and over the guard rail, ending the life of Christopher Simons. John has fear in his eyes, seeing the death of his cellmate. The Archangels moves toward John to comfort him. Unlike

Christopher, John you asked for forgiveness and turned your attention towards God.

You asked for a way and God has a plan for you. A mission, just for you. All you have to do is take my hand and come with us. John stands up and says yes Lord, with tears coming down his face.

At this time the Archangels, Ms. Montez, and John William Strong disappear. Gabriel appears in a high school in Norway. As he stands in this classroom; a bright light suddenly appears in the classroom. It causes the teacher and students to run out of the room.

All but one young lady is sitting up front in the classroom. Sitting in the back of the classroom is a young woman who appears to be mentally anywhere other than the classroom and is not moved or phased by any instruction given by the teacher.

EPISODE 6 – THE OUTCOME

Gabriel appears in front of the young woman, the other students and teacher run screaming out of the classroom. Without looking up she simply says, I do not believe in GOD and why are you here?

Why should I help you? Gabriel moves forward and sits down. GOD did not kill your father my child, it was his time. Again, without raising her head, if GOD wants me to help on this mission, why did he not save my father? Gabriel says, Ruth, GOD does not negotiate. You have the free will to stay here or come with me. All I ask is that you take my hand before you make your decision.

Ruth says whatever, I will not change my mind and extends her hand. Gabriel touches Ruth's hand and she sees her father, grandmother, and all of her relatives who passed on, Laughing, playing and at peace.

She cries and falls to the floor. I did not know, I did not know, forgive me. Gabriel says, just by asking the deed it is done. It is time to go child. Gabriel lifts her from the floor and disappears. Just as the Principal and teacher opens the classroom door looking around in amazement, that the classroom is empty.

Xavier and Devlin reappear on a boat off the coastline of Norway. Xavier tells Devlin to call the General. Devlin looks at him, if I call him, he will not be happy. Xavier says we have no choice, call him! Devlin goes into a Trans like state and a man appears with the battle marks of war on his face.

Why did you summon me? You have no authority to call the Army of Darkness to war. Everything that has been written to come will come. You have no power to change any of that. Xavier, we may command some of the dark warriors. I must end this battle and I need more powerful warriors.

Devlin says, if we fail our punishment will be shared by you since we have invited you to this assignment. General Razen puts a knife against the neck of Devlin and laughs. I should cut out your black soul for getting me involved in this mess. I will dispatch two legions for you to command but remember this is your mess. Do not summon me again or I will kill you both! He disappears.

Michael arrives in the Desert with David and Jantai. He waves his hand, and the dry Desert sand turns into a beautiful Oasis. At the edge of the clearing is a temple. Michael moves forward towards the temple. Walking behind him now are all the Archangels, David, Jantai, Cindy and Samantha (twins), Ms. Montez, John William Strong, and Ruth.

Xavier and Devlin chant to locate the Archangels and the chosen with a sadistic smile they say together Eden. Michael leads the group into the temple, once his foot crosses the doorway the temple lights up. The beauty and wonderment of the temple makes the children with the two adults yell, AWESOME!

Michael tells the chosen and Raphael to follow him. Gabriel, Ariel, Azarel, and Uriel stay outside the temple and let no one come in, you will have company soon. Gabriel leads his group outside and makes ready to repel any attack.

Michael tells Raphael this is the second line of defense. I trust you to wait here and protect this area. Raphael laughs and says, time for some fun! Michael escorts the children, Ms. Montez, and John Strong to a room down the hallway.

In the room he places the chosen in a circle and asks if they know the 91st Psalm, they all say, yes. Michael tells them all to hold hands, have a seat on the floor, and repeat the 91st Psalm aloud repeatedly.

No matter what you hear or see, do not stop. I will place protection over you, nothing and no one will harm you.

As the children, Ms. Montez and John Strong recite the 91st Psalm, Michael leaves out of the room. Michael enters the hallway and turns to the doorway where the children are and touches the bottom, up and around the arch of the doorway, placing a protective seal. He stands in the hallway with his sword drawn between his legs. He says, Lucifer send your best.

Xavier and Devlin arrive in Eden and see Gabriel and the Archangels positioned outside the temple. Xavier tells Devlin to attack, and I will enter the temple with a small group of men, while the Archangels are busy. The army of darkness appears behind them with blood in their eyes ready to kill them. With one word, Devlin advances the massive army of unholy souls and says, kill.

Gabriel raises his trumpet, and a noise comes out that is heard all over the world. The small band of angels' advance and prepare for battle.

At this time a bright light and explosion lands in front of the advancing army, of unholy servants. Jupiel appears in white and gold armor, with wings so large and beautiful it can block out the sun. She says behold the army of the Lord and fear the coming of the King. Suddenly, thousands of angels with shining swords appear and cut through the army of darkness. Jupiel eyes Devlin and makes her way towards her.

Gabriel tells the Archangels to back up and hold this position so no one can enter the temple. Unfortunately, Gabriel did not see Xavier and thirty of his demon warriors have breached the temple. Once in the temple, Xavier sees Raphael standing in their way.

Raphael without a second thought attacks while reciting the 23rd Psalm as he cuts through the demons. Xavier seeing his opportunity heads toward the back hallway with fifteen of his demons. Xavier sees Michael waiting for him and says what hope do you have? You are outnumbered, give up the chosen.

Michael laughs and tell Xavier remember the person who you call master once tasted the foot that will soon crush your neck. Come taste the power given by the one GOD, my father.

Michael moves forward with speed, force, and deadly accuracy as body parts of the demon's fly. Xavier moves forward to fight Michael. Gabriel and the other Archangels are now fighting outside the temple entrance. Gabriel laughs as he hears Raphael inside cutting the demons down like trees.

In the distance, Jupiel and Devlin are in a fierce battle on ground, and in the air. Anyone that is in their path are knocked down backwards by the intensity of the blows. Devlin makes a fatal mistake and lounges forward, thinking Jupiel is stunned. She is immediately decapitated.

Jupiel without a second thought joins Gabriel to help him repel the demons from the temple entrance. Michael kills the last of the demons in the hallway and battles Xavier.

While Michael is fighting Xavier, he sees Raphael kill the last demon and rejoices. Michael yells, Raphael it is not over! Lucifer appears and knocks Raphael into the wall.

Xavier laughs at the sight of the Archangel flying into the wall by Lucifer.

In the split-second Xavier turned his attention away from Michael and he slashes Xavier with his sword. Xavier drops his sword and Michael walks pass him toward Lucifer. Meantime behind Michael, Xavier body falls to the ground broken up into two pieces.

Michael and Lucifer go blow to blow. Neither seem to make any headway. A teenage boy appears in a white suit immaculately dressed from head to toe. Lucifer yells, it is not over! You will not win! The boy lifts his head toward Lucifer and waves his hand, as of today it is over. Lucifer disappears.

The boy smiles at Raphael and Michael. They drop to their knees. Michael tells GOD, father I could have destroyed the evil one. GOD now appears as an old woman and explains, no Michael it is not his time and only the time written will the dark one be destroyed. Michael your battle cannot be over. But soon my child you will be the witness to his end.

GOD turns without a strain and is heard in the minds of the chosen, come. GOD then turns toward the doorway of the temple and blows. The demons outside disappear. GOD tells Jupiel and her army of angels to return home my children. Jupiel and the angels return to heaven, Gabriel and the other Archangels come inside the temple. Michael, the Archangels, and the chosen kneel before GOD.

Each one sees something different as GOD speaks. A little boy, a girl, an older woman, a man, an Asian man, a Black man, etc... Each vision of GOD is different to each person. GOD extends his hands over the chosen. Ms. Montez and John Strong your journey is not over. As you feel my love, I give you the power to move mountains, the strength, and wisdom to speak the truth.

Go out into the world and bless others. Lead them to the truth and tell them I Love them. Understand they have free will to choose, but time grows short for my son will return soon.

GOD turns to Michael and the Archangels your journey is not over. You will accompany them all over the world, spreading my word. The negative forces will try to stop you, but my love will always be with you.

They all smile as a light surrounds them all. One child says, it is like being hugged and tickled simultaneously. Awesome! GOD disappears.

Michael looks at the Archangels and the chosen by God and says okay let us go we have work to do!

IS THIS THE END. OR IS IT THE BEGINNING??

ABOUT THE AUTHOR

Parrish Whitaker is a first-time novelist who through research and life experience has inspired him to write this book. His interest in Christianity and belief that there are still good people in the world is the reason why this book was written. To inspire those who have similar beliefs. Encourage you when times of trouble come, you can overcome any obstacle when you place God at the head of your life. Enjoy as you read this wonderful work.

Made in the USA
Middletown, DE
12 September 2021